Walt Disney's
Pooh's
Adventures
with Words

wiggly / wavy

E. P. DUTTON | NEW YORK

Table of

carrots

KeRiTs

Contents

chimney

attic

ceiling

cupboard

curtain

shelf

stairs

closet

window

fireplace

floor

rug

The House of Pooh

Just as Winnie-the-Pooh was moving the last piece of furniture outside so that he could begin cleaning inside, his work was interrupted by Loud Grumbly Noises coming from his stomach—noises that told him he was a Very-Hungry-Bear-in-Need-of-Lunch.

sheet

blanket

quilt

bed

mirror

chest

pillow

armchair

mattress

bell

table

stool

flowerpot

door

drawer

chair

clock

HUNNY

honeypot

candle

picture

vase

One Spring Morning

tulips

daffodils

daisy(ies)

Piglet was looking for violets. He found . . .

dandelions

bluebells

primroses

snapdragons

poppy(ies)

buttercups

foxgloves

pansy(ies)

lady's slippers

sweet williams

8

"We've been looking for you all morning," said Pooh huffing and puffing as he climbed the hill.

"Why?" asked Piglet.

"We were afraid you were lost," said Rabbit.

"That's silly. I knew where I was," said Piglet. "I've been looking for violets."

tiger lily(ies)

roses

marigolds

violets

petunias

Rabbit's Friends and Relations

After Pooh had a nice visit with Rabbit and an even nicer snack, he became stuck in Rabbit's front door when he tried to leave.

"This is what comes from not making front doors big enough," said Pooh crossly.

"No!" said Rabbit. "This is what comes from eating too much honey." Luckily for both, Rabbit's friends and relations came to help.

doe

fawn

porcupine

raccoon

newt

skunk

frog

mouse

mole

chipmunk

squirrel

buck

beaver

turtle

snail

RABBIT'S
HOWSE

11

One Summer Day

One fine summer day Christopher Robin and his friends packed a picnic lunch. After eating they all played games. Everyone had a wonderful time—even some uninvited guests.

walking stick

picnic basket

thermos

grasshopper

cup

juice

spiderweb

butterfly

leaf hopper

spider

Things That Fall from Trees

In the Hundred Acre Wood there is a tall pine tree which Tigger climbed. As he discovered when he reached the top, Tiggers are very good at climbing in every direction—except *down!*

apple tree

maple tree

pine tree

tree stump

vine

log

fern

boulder

grass

stone

moss

14

oak tree

chestnut tree

bush

rock

wildflowers

acorn   walnut   seed pod   chestnut   pine cone

These are also things that fall from trees.   15

One Fall Evening

On Halloween Eve Pooh said to Piglet, "Let's put on scary masks and frighten Kanga. And then we'll tell her who we really are."

Frankenstein mask

werewolf mask

Indian corn

witch's costume

candy apples

broom

jack-o'-lantern

"trick or treat" bag

So that is what they did. Only Kanga did not seem very frightened at all. Then up pounced Tigger right behind Pooh and Piglet. That was really scary!

ghost costume

autumn leaves

pumpkin

gourds

17

What Happened on Windsday

One blustery day the wind blew down the big chestnut tree. Owl's house, which happened to be in it, came down. Then everyone came round to help Owl with Repairs and Building.

wagon

sawhorse

screwdriver

saw

drill

screw

file

tool box

ladder

board

nail

pliers

hammer

wrench

bolt

nut

19

One Winter Afternoon

Everyone wanted to have a Christmas party. But no one could decide where to have it. Pooh had a nice fireplace at *his* house. And Kanga had just baked seven kinds of cookies at *hers*. Then Eeyore said, "Of course, *my* house is much too small and humble for a party." And that was when everyone decided to have the party at Eeyore's house.

icicle

ribbon

wreath

mistletoe

poinsettia

holly

cranberries

sled

present

tracks

popcorn

ice

snowball

garland

ornament

Christmas tree

snowman

candy cane

gingerbreadmen cookies

snow

wrapping paper

21

Little Smackerels—Honey

Pooh's favorite food is made by honey bees. Worker bees gather nectar from flowers and store it in honeycombs inside the hive. Bees work very, very hard. Well, most bees do.

honeycomb

CLOVER

ORANGE

drone bee

queen bee

worker bee

beehive

flower

pollen

honeybee

Maple Syrup

Late in Winter, Christopher Robin and his friends get up early in the morning to collect sap from the maple trees. The sap is boiled down to make maple syrup. Pooh likes his maple syrup with or without pancakes.

branch

maple tree

trunk

spout

sap

maple syrup

bucket

sled

corks

funnel

bottles

23

Rabbit Makes a Sustaining Soup

When Rabbit woke up that morning, he knew that this was a day for Making Things . . . making plans, making statements, making sure that everyone knew what Rabbit thought about this and about that.

And to get through such a big, busy day, Rabbit needed to eat something sustaining—something full of vitamins!

So the first thing that Rabbit did that day was make a pot of vegetable soup.

pot holder

ladle

spice rack

scale

frying pan

kettle

herbs

saucepan

stove

lid

grater

cabbage

onions

colander

pepper

knife

celery

peeler

potato masher

garlic

peas

alphabet noodles

Rabbit's Garden

One day Rabbit was watering his garden when he came across a hole. "I wonder where this hole goes" he puzzled. "Holes don't belong in gardens. Only growing things belong here."

Little did Rabbit realize that Gopher was growing something too.

sunflowers

beans

tomatoes

peppers

cucumber

brussels sprouts

eelbarrow

eggplant

watering can

celery

trowel

cauliflower

lettuce

hoe

rot

radish

topsoil

roots

earthworm

potatoes

subsoil

rock

mushrooms

25

water table

Blizzards and Whatnot

rainy

"It's not much of a house, but it keeps me dry."

windy

"After all, we can't all have houses!"

snowy

"If it snows much longer, I shall start to complain."

sunny

"Don't blame me if it starts to rain."

Clothes for a Windy Day

cap

sweater

scarf

jacket

rain hat

umbrella

rain coat

boots

Clothes for a Rainy Day

shirt

pants

socks

shoes

Clothes for a Sunny Day

hat

earmuffs

muffler

snowsuit

mittens

Clothes for a Snowy Day

Hailstorm

"You don't go out during a hailstorm."

27

Birds

parrot

stork

eagle

heron

puffin

dove

ostrich

hummingbird

blue jay

peacock

kiwi

crane

28

cardinal

cockatoo

robin

swan

pelican

.gfisher

pheasant

flamingo

penguin

woodpecker

29

At Roundabout Farm

Roundabout Farm is not far from Christopher Robin's house. Sometimes Christopher Robin and Pooh go there together. Then, after they say hello to the new baby chicks and feed an apple to the horse, they climb up to the hayloft and talk about Important Things.

scarecrow

wagon

cornfield

fence

dog

Round-About Farm

mailbox

puppy

farmhouse

porch

windmill

weather vane

silo

barn

pickup truck

well

haystack

tractor

crow

pasture

plow

Farm Animals

pitchfork

bucket

rope

cat

horse

cow

calf

cowbell

gosling

goose

pig

kitten

foal

piglets

hayloft

horseshoe

rooster

stall

halter

bull

pump

goat

sheep

kid

lamb

trough

chicken

milk can

chicks

duck

duckling

33

Down By the Sea

On the day that everyone went to the seashore, Roo asked Tigger, "Can Tiggers Swim?" "Of course Tiggers can swim," said Tigger. "Tiggers can do anything!"

"But," he added as he jumped into the water, "splashing is what Tiggers do best."

lighthouse

pier

ocean

buoy

driftwood

anchor

wave

bathing suit

inner tube

beach towel

horseshoe crab

sandpiper

conch sh

cowrie shell

hermit crab

pebble

mussel shell

coral

seagull

dune

shovel

sand castle

sea horse

pail

seaweed

beach ball

crab

scallop shell

sand dollar

sea urchin

sea anemone

tidepool

barnacles

clam

starfish

35

A Visit to the Zoo

Everyone went to visit their favorite animals at the zoo. Tigger saw a tiger. Christopher Robin fed peanuts to the elephant. Eeyore cheered up when he saw that the rhinoceros was much more wrinkled than he.

Pooh found the Heffalumps and Woozle cage. Luckily the Heffalumps and Woozles weren't in. They are so huge, so fierce, and so dangerous that Pooh was bound to be quite frightened.

gazelle

rhinoceros

leopard

panther

snake

tiger

lion

elephant

monkey

giraffe

zebra

camel

hippopotamus

bear

WOOZLE
HEFFA-
LUMPS

alligator

gorilla

Song and Dance

"Let's have some fun," said Kanga. "I'll play the piano, Pooh can hum one of his hums, and everyone else can play his favorite instruments."

Poor Rabbit! He really didn't feel like dancing—not with Tigger, that is!

drumsticks

cymbal

guitar

drums

trumpet

tambourine

saxophone

banjo

harmonica   trombone

Kanga's Bake Day

Something that smelled absolutely wonderful was in the air. Christopher Robin and Pooh followed the scent until they came to Kanga's kitchen.

muffin tin

spatula

ove[n]

cake pan

pie

cookie jar

cake

cookies

cupcakes

apron

rolling pin

funnel

batter

spices

milk

mixing bowl

cookie sheet

dough

eggs

flour

measuring spoon

nuts

measuring cup

nutcracker

Washday at Kanga's

Washday at Kanga's house is a very busy day. It is the day that Kanga washes all the clothes, and little Roo too!

st

handkerchief

pajamas

overalls

soapsuds

bathrobe

washcloth

towel

apron

clothes basket

soap

bucket

box of soap

washboard

hespins

sponge

bath mat

Parts of the Body

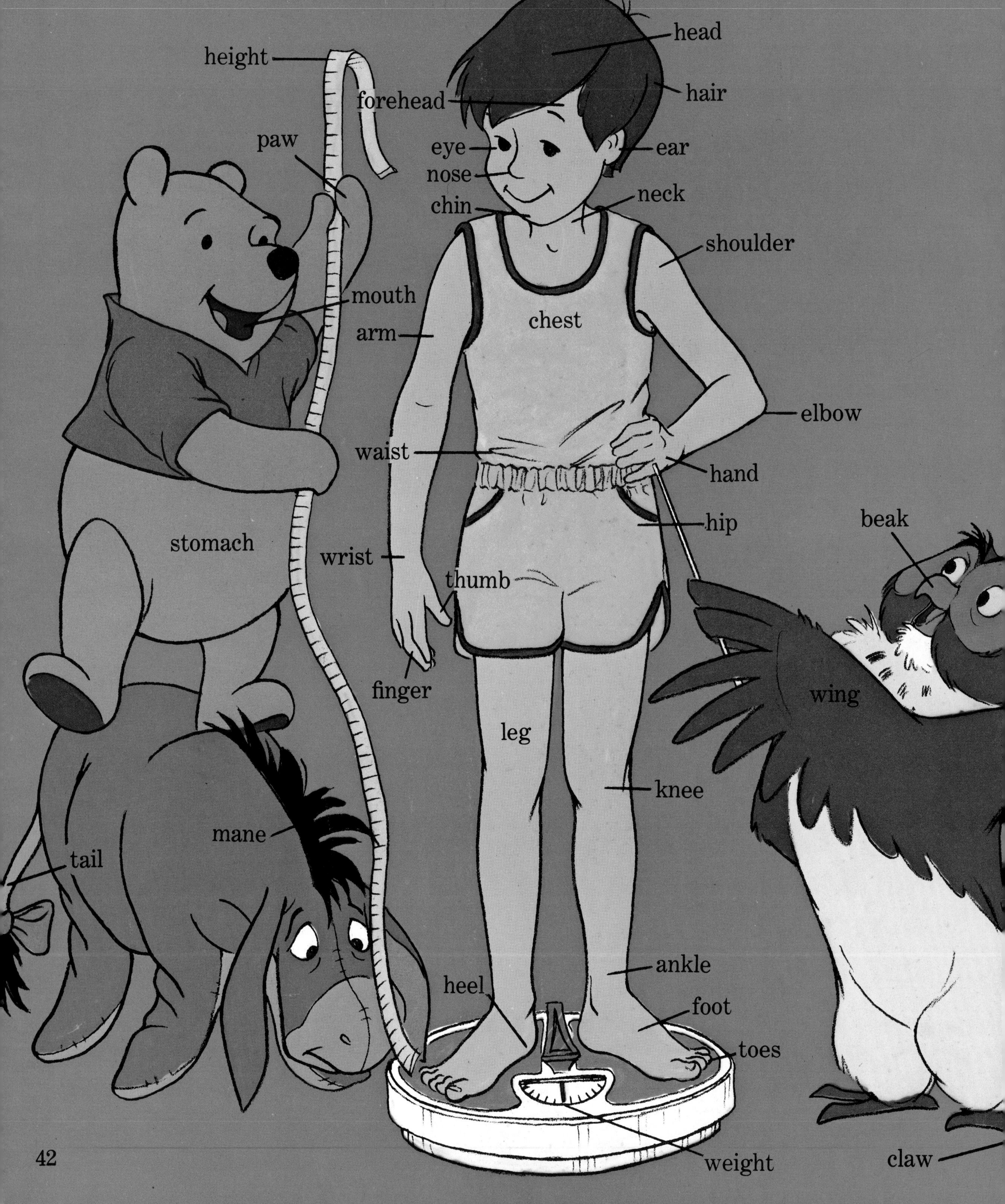

height

paw

forehead

head

hair

eye

ear

nose

neck

chin

shoulder

chest

mouth

arm

waist

elbow

stomach

hand

wrist

hip

thumb

beak

finger

wing

tail

mane

leg

knee

heel

ankle

foot

toes

weight

claw

42

Colors

TIGGER: "What are you doing, Piglet?"
PIGLET: "I'm painting my fence."
TIGGER: "Why are you using so many colors?"
PIGLET: "I couldn't make up my mind which I liked best!"

brown

purple

red

pink

white

blue

green

orange

gray

yellow

black

43

Numbers

"What do Tiggers like for lunch?" asked Pooh. "Tiggers like *everything*," answered Tigger. But the more food Tigger tasted, the more things he found that Tiggers *don't* like!

Tiggers like everything except honey.

1 jar of honey

Tiggers like everything except honey and apples.

2 apples

Tiggers like everything except honey, apples, and cucumber sandwiches.

3 cucumber sandwiches

Tiggers like everything except honey, apples, cucumber sandwiches, and carrots.

4 carrots

Tiggers like everythin except honey, apples cucumber sandwiche carrots, and tea.

5 cups of tea

At last Tigger tried some of Roo's Strengthening Medicine. To everyone's surprise, Tigger liked it. In fact, that medicine made Tigger feel bouncier than ever.

Eeyore's Alphabet

One day Piglet saw Eeyore staring at three sticks on the ground.
"What are those three sticks for?" asked Piglet.
"This is not three sticks," said Eeyore. "This is an 'A'."
"Oh," said Piglet.
"Not 'O'," said Eeyore. "A!"

acorn

bicycle

clown

doll

Eeyore

fish

grapes

house

ice cream

46

J

jar

K kiss

L

licorice

M moon

N nest

Owl

P popcorn

Q quilt

rocking horse

S seal

T

train

U

unicorn

valentine

W

whistle

X xylophone

Y

yo-yo

Z

zig-zags

Arts and Crafts

Everyone is in an artistic mood today. They all get out their materials and do artwork. Since Eeyore is the most patient he gets to be the model.

easel

model

watercolors

paint brush

wastebasket

blackboard

paper

clay

scissors

paste

chalk eraser

paper maché

chalk

string

ink

tape

ruler

eraser

pen

triangle

pencil

pencil sharpener

Rabbit's Family Tree

cousins

nephew

niece

Rabbit

sister

brother-in-law

brother

uncle

aunt

father

mother

grandfather

grandmother

Trains

switch tower

signal

caboose

sleeping car

tracks

steam locomotive

gondola car

monorail

flat car

boxcar

engine

tank car

railroad crossing signal

trolley

Cars and Trucks

jeep

van

billboard

ambulance

garbage truck

station wagon

street

fire engine

race car

tow truck

100 ACRE WOODS

station

ticket window

platform

stop sign

dump truck

bulldozer

payloader

police car

traffic light

bus

mail truck

taxi

tractor-trailer

fire hydrant

convertible

51

Boats and Ships

speedboat

ocean liner

hydrofoil

Hovercraft

tugboat

yacht

fishing

pirate ship

Viking ship

submarine

sailboa

52

canoe

rowboat

Planes

biplane

blimp

helicopter

jet liner

private plane

space shuttle

U.F.O.

sea plane

supersonic transport

jet

One day Pooh came upon Tigger sitting in a box making growly noises.
Pooh: "Why are you sitting in a box?"
Tigger: "Im flying my airplane through the sky."
Pooh: "It doesn't look like an airplane to me."
Tigger: "Huh! There are all different kinds of planes. But homemade is the best!"

Doing Things

looking

smelling

touching

WET PAINT

tasting

talking

listening

still talking

yawning

still talking

sleeping

floating

popping

falling

landing

bouncing

running

hiding

SURPRISE!

55

Long Ago and Far Away

Some days Christopher Robin finds a nice cozy spot. There he sits with his favorite book—the book of magical stories that all begin with "Once Upon a Time."

Daytime

"Pooh," said Christopher Robin, "did you know that there is a pot of gold at the end of every rainbow?"

"Oh, bother," said Pooh. "I was hoping there was a pot of honey there instead."

Nighttime

One night Pooh thought he heard a strange noise just outside his door. "WORRA-WORRA-WORRA-WORRA," went the noise. And Pooh found it very hard to sleep.

star

moon

bat

nightcap

lantern

nightshirt

firefly

slippers

HOOT

CHIRP

CROAK

shadow

frog

Very Nearly Tea Time

Just as Owl was sitting down to have some tea one afternoon, he began to think, "If a bear named Pooh isn't standing right outside my door trying to think of a reason to come in and stay for tea, my name isn't Owl."

And of course, Owl's name was Owl, and a bear named Pooh was standing right outside his door trying to think of a reason to go in and stay for tea.

pitcher

tea pot

napkin

plate

glass

tray

cup

spoon

saucer

biscuits

sugar bowl

fork

creamer

table cloth

muffin

cheese

coasters

crackers

butt

60

knife

Pooh's Sweet Snacks

Here are some other sweet things that Pooh likes to eat besides honey.

apple

banana

grapes

plum

peach

pineapple

pear

orange

cherries

strawberries

blueberries

raspberries

watermelon

core

rind

seeds

peel

pit

Happy Birthday, Eeyore!

There was a surprise birthday party for Eeyore, and everybody was there. When Eeyore saw the cake and the hats and all of those balloons, he started looking.

He looked to the left of him. He looked to the right of him. "What are you looking for?" asked Christopher Robin.

"I'm looking for someone else who is having a birthday," said Eeyore. "Such a wonderful party can't be for me."

"It is for you," everyone shouted. "HAPPY BIRTHDAY, EEYORE!"

party hat

noise maker

birthday card

pun

paper plate

ribbon

present

62